JAMAICA

HISPANIOLA

For Jack Haswell Bailey – Midshipman, Mugwump and Hornswoggler

1 3 5 7 9 10 8 6 4 2

Copyright © Peter Haswell 1995

Peter Haswell has asserted his right under the Copyright, Designs
and Patents Act, 1988 to be identified as the author and
illustrator of this work

First published in the United Kingdom 1995
by The Bodley Head Children's Books
Random House, 20 Vauxhall Bridge Road, London SW1V 2SA

Random House Australia (Pty) Limited
20 Alfred Street, Milsons Point, Sydney
New South Wales 2061, Australia

Random House New Zealand Limited
18 Poland Road, Glenfield
Auckland 10, New Zealand

Random House South Africa (Pty) Limited
PO Box 337, Bergvlei 2012, South Africa

Random House UK Limited Reg. No. 954009

A CIP catalogue record for this book is available
from the British Library

ISBN 0 37031877 3

Printed in Hong Kong

PETER HASWELL

CAPTAIN PRUE

AND HER SCURVY CREW

CAPTAIN PRUE DANGEROUS DAN SIMPLE SID NIFFY NED BIG BAD BART

THE BODLEY HEAD
LONDON

NE morning, a scurvy crew of rough and rascally pirates came clumping along a quay. As they walked, they groused and griped about their captain.

"She made me take a bath!" complained Niffy Ned. "And it's taken me years to pong like this."

"She makes us eat healthy foods all the time," whined Simple Sid.

"Aar," moaned Dangerous Dan, "I'm sick o' sprouts, fed up wi' fruit, cheesed off wi' cheese and bored wi' blooming beans!"

"Come on, lads," said Big Bad Bart. "Let's go and drown our sorrows in The Rapscallion's Return."

Still muttering, the motley mob entered
THE RAPSCALLION'S RETURN.

Once inside, they were in for a nasty surprise.

Sitting at a table were their rivals – Captain Blackbucket's crew of raucous rowdies.

"Avast!" exclaimed Blackbucket. "Swash my buckle! If it isn't Captain Prue's namby-pamby crew! Aren't they pretty boys, then!"

At this, there was a gleeful gust of giggles, guffaws, snorts and sniggers.

Captain Prue's scurvy crew beat a hasty retreat!

Gloomily, the pirates shambled back along the quay towards their ship, the Peggy Sue.

"Lads," said Big Bad Bart, "it's no good. We've got to do something. And it's got to be evil, foul and filthy. We've got our reputations to think about."

"We could pick our noses in the post office," suggested Simple Sid. "That would be foul and filthy."

"No," said Big Bad Bart. "We're going to be more cunning than that. We're going to bide our time 'til the ship's at sea. Then, when the Captain least expects it – we be going to MUTINY!"

The Peggy Sue was sailing, way out on the ocean.

Up in the crow's nest, Prue was looking through her spyglass.

This is what Prue saw through her spyglass

"By thunder!" she exclaimed. "I can see black storm clouds heading this way. We'd better make the ship ready at once."

Quickly, Prue clambered down to the deck.

At that moment, the scurvy crew came lumbering up the ladder and clumping along the deck.

"Captain," thundered Big Bad Bart. "We be going to MUTINY!"

"Aye," grinned Niffy Ned, "we be going to throw you overboard!"

"Hold hard, lads," gasped Prue. Her mind raced. A mutiny! What was she to do? Then she had an idea. "Before you mutiny, lads," she said, "let me cook you one last dinner. And I'll make it a meal to remember."

And so Captain Prue went down into the ship's galley and cooked a meal. And as she cooked, she kept looking out of the porthole.

The scurvy crew sat down to a mighty meal.

"That dinner was disgusting!" exclaimed Dangerous Dan. "Just the way I like it! Now, let's go up and grab the captain!"

Back on deck, Prue was steering the ship as fast it would go towards the port. The sea was beginning to heave and the storm was almost upon them.

Suddenly, her scurvy crew came charging up the ladder armed with pots and pans and all manner of kitchen utensils.

"Captain!" they cried, "You're done for!"

"Whoa, lads!" cried Prue. "Don't be hasty!"

But the rebellious rabble seized their captain and dragged her towards the ship's rail.

"Bye, bye, Captain!" yelled the pirates. "Cheerio!"

AT THAT MOMENT THE STORM STRUCK!

The ship pitched and plunged.

EEEEEK!

Which hat belongs on which head?

The crew became disgustingly seasick.

And while all that was going on …

Captain Prue steered the ship safely back into port.

A FEW DAYS LATER

On the ship's deck, Captain Prue was giving her scurvy crew dancing lessons.

After dancing, Prue went back to steering the ship.

But the crew started muttering among themselves.

"We don't need dancing lessons," grumbled Big Bad Bart. "We need fighting, cheating and fibbing lessons."

"She'll be reading us fairy stories next," sneered Dangerous Dan.

"I like fairy stories," said Simple Sid,

"Right, lads," said Niffy Ned. "You know what we've got to do. We've got to MUTINY!"

"We tried that before and it didn't work," said Big Bad Bart.

"We'll try again," said Niffy Ned. "Come on, men, LET'S GRAB HER!"

The pirates dashed along the deck and made a grab for Prue, but she was too quick for them and jumped into the rigging.

"Hold hard, lads," shouted Captain Prue. "You've forgotten something!"

But the big, bumbling pirates rushed to the rigging and clambered up after her …

"Lads," cried Captain Prue as she swung herself up, higher and higher, "you've forgotten something!"

"Lads," wailed Captain Prue as she edged out on the yardarm, "you've forgotten something!"

At last, Prue found herself at the front of the ship. She crawled out along the bowsprit and stopped. She could go no further.

"Lads," she gasped weakly, "you've forgotten something."

"Aha, Captain," called Niffy Ned. "Gotcha! Now then, don't move – we be sending Simple Sid along to grab you."

"Lads," croaked Prue, "you've forgotten that I'm the only one who brings you cocoa in bed and darns your socks and makes you birthday cakes with icing and candles on and teaches you joined-up writing and sings you lullabies when you can't sleep at night for fear of monsters and ghosts …"

" … but most of all you've forgotten that I'm the only one who can steer the ship. And if you look ahead you'll see that we're heading for disaster!"

This is the disaster
the ship was heading for.

EEEEEK!

"Er … help!" wailed Niffy Ned.

"Oooh … I feel funny!" groaned Dangerous Dan.

"I want to go home," squeaked Simple Sid.

"Beg pardon, Captain," said Big Bad Bart. "Not wishing to put you to any trouble. But, please would you mind steering the ship for us?"

So Prue crawled back along the bowsprit… took the ship's wheel …

and, once more, steered them all to safety.

Her scurvy crew blinked with relief.

"And now," said Captain Prue, "if you promise to be good boys, I'll give you a special treat."

"We promise! We promise!" chorused the crew.

And so Prue read them a fairy story.

Under Captain's orders, the scurvy crew were hard at
work cleaning the ship. And as they worked, they muttered
murderously among themselves,

"I'm sick o' rubbing and scrubbing," grunted Dangerous Dan.
"I vote we mutiny again."

"Aar," snorted Niffy Ned. "We'll do for her in the most
fearsome way possible."

"Right," said Big Bad Bart with a cunning wink. "We'll *trick*
her into admitting what scares her most."

They found Prue polishing the cannon.

"Captain," cried Big Bad Bart, "we've decided to mutiny again. And this time we're going to *scare* you to death!"

"So tell us the truth," chortled Dangerous Dan. "If we stuffed you into the cannon and shot you out to sea, would that scare you?"

Prue thought about that …

It sounded ghastly!

"No," said Prue, "that wouldn't scare me a bit."

"Oh," said the crew, "that's a pity. Well … er … we'd better think again shipmates …"

"I've got it!" exclaimed Big Bad Bart. "What if we blindfolded you and made you walk the plank?"

Prue thought about that …

It sounded horrid!

"No," said Prue, "that wouldn't scare me either."

"Oh," groaned the pirates. "Now what do we do?"

"I know!" gloated Niffy Ned. "What if we threw you to the sharks? Would that scare you?"

Prue thought about that …

"No," she said, "that wouldn't scare me."

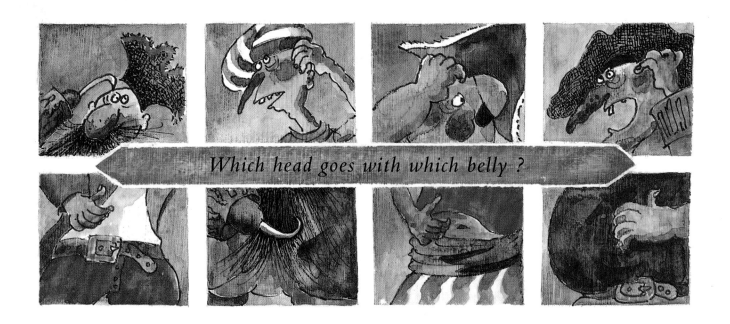

Which head goes with which belly?

The pirates scratched their heads and their bellies and looked dejected.

Then Simple Sid piped up. "All right Captain Cleversides," he said, "you tell us what *would* scare you."

"I'm not telling," said Prue.

"Not fair! Boo! What a rotten sport!" shouted the pirates.

"Oh, all right," said Prue. "What would really scare me …"

"Yes? What?" begged the crew.

" … would be if you rowed off in the ship's boat and left me all alone on this great, big, creaky, spooky ship. That would really scare me!"

"Got her!" roared the rollicking rabble of rascally (rather stupid) rotters as they jumped into the ship's boat.

"Bye, bye! Good riddance! We'll send you a postcard!" they shouted gleefully.

Then they headed off towards the distant shore.

And while her scurvy crew rowed away, Captain Prue took the wheel of the Peggy Sue and set course for the distant horizon.

The scurvy crew were once more on the quay.

"I'm starving," groaned Big Bad Bart.
"Me too," moaned Simple Sid.
"I could eat anything," whined Dangerous Dan.
"Even healthy food," sighed Simple Sid.

At that moment an old sea salt came lurching along the quay.
"I be looking for Captain Prue," he croaked. "Have you heard tell of her?"

"Captain Prue?" cried the pirates. "Why, she was our captain,
but we mutinied and so she went off and left us."

"What would you do if your captain came back?"
asked the ancient sailor.

"We'd never mutiny again," cried the pirates.
"We'd scrub the decks, practise dancing and always
be nice to our dear captain."

"In that case," said the old sea salt …